P9-DDR-804

Best wishes!

Larry and Bob

By Karen Schaufeld

Illustrations by Kurt Schwarz

Keep the color in your life!

Quidne Press

Smart Books for Smart Kids

Published by Quidne Press

Library of Congress Control Number: 2016938299

Illustrated by Kurt Schwarz

Quidne Press
P.O. Box 6266, Leesburg, VA 20178
www.Quidnepress.org

Hardcover:
ISBN - 9 780997 229905

To Grace —
who sailed across the ocean
to discover a new life.

Once upon a time, there was a Bald Eagle named Larry. He lived in a nest that was six feet wide in a tall tree next to a broad river. His snow-frosted nest held a pile of fish bones, the feathers and down of smaller birds, and one large egg.

Bob was a Smallmouth Bass. He lived in the river below Larry's nest. While Larry watched over his egg in the nest, Bob was hard at work protecting 19,003 eggs nestled in a rock nest. Whenever Bob thought about launching the young fish into the big river, he got a little teary.

One day, feeling hungry, Larry stretched his wings wide and swooped low over the sparkling river. He saw the flash of silver and the flick of fins below him. “Mmmmm, lunch,” Larry thought, as he skimmed the crest of a small wave, stretched his talons into the water, and grabbed onto the sides of a delicious fresh fish.

Bob had swum up to peek at the sky when he saw the edge of a shadow from the corner of his eye. Suddenly, Bob felt sharp stings in his sides as he was lifted up out of the water. Powerless, he saw his own shadow clutched in a bird's talons reflected below him as he skimmed over the waves. Bob was frightened and confused. He looked up and saw the curved beak of an eagle.

Even though Bob was scared, he still noticed the strangest sights as he flew through the air.

His entire rivery world sliced through endless hills and valleys and flowed through a wide sweep of trees that were the fluorescent green of emerging leaves.

Larry dropped Bob from his talons into his nest. A puff of down rose up as Bob hit the nest floor. Bob gasped for air. His gills were rimmed red from the effort. As Larry's beak arched down ready to begin his lunch, Bob exclaimed, "NOOOOOOOOOOOOO! CAN'T WE TALK THIS OVER?!"

Larry tilted his head in surprise. His food had never spoken to him before.

Bob took his chance. “I can tell you are a caring eagle, doing your best to provide for your little one,” gesturing with his fin to the egg beside him. “I have a lot of little ones to care for too. Perhaps, dad to dad, you could just let me get back to my job?”

Larry was still wrapping his head around talking to his food. Slowly, he responded, “I wouldn’t be a very good dad if I didn’t feed my family, and YOU are food.

“Maybe, in exchange for your life, you could show me the hiding places of the other fish?”

Bob thought only for a second before stating, "No, it would be against my principles to help you find other fish. It's not that I'm against you eating," reasoned Bob, "it's just that I, too, have work to do.

"I won't deny you your meal, although I had hoped to die a little less painfully. But, if you let me go, I will send my young ones off, put my fish affairs in order, and then meet you one year from today at the rock where you caught me."

Larry looked around for his mate. She would surely think he was crazy to talk to a fish, much less consider letting the fish go! And, even though he was suspicious of the promise that Bob made, Larry was feeling magnanimous. He decided that he, Larry, the most noble of all birds, could release this poor fish to finish his fish work.

Gently this time, Larry picked up Bob in his talons. He swooped low over the river near the flat rock where he first spotted Bob and dropped him into the water. Larry flew off shouting, "I will see you here in one year!" Bob poked his head above the surface of the river, tipped a fin to Larry, and dove down.

Over the following months, Bob's days were filled with fanning his nest, carefully corralling his newly hatched fry, and scouting the water for predators. Bob hovered over his little ones and fretted with each loss whenever one strayed too far away and was picked off by other fish.

Bob saw his world differently since Larry had returned him to the river. On the one fin, he felt a lot smaller since he'd seen that the world was a lot bigger than he had ever dreamed. But, on the other fin, he realized that his job as a father was so important that he had convinced a mighty eagle to change his lunch plan!

Sometimes, Bob peered up through the glassy, undulating surface of the water and saw Larry fly over with some other unlucky fish. He dreaded the day he would be making that journey with Larry.

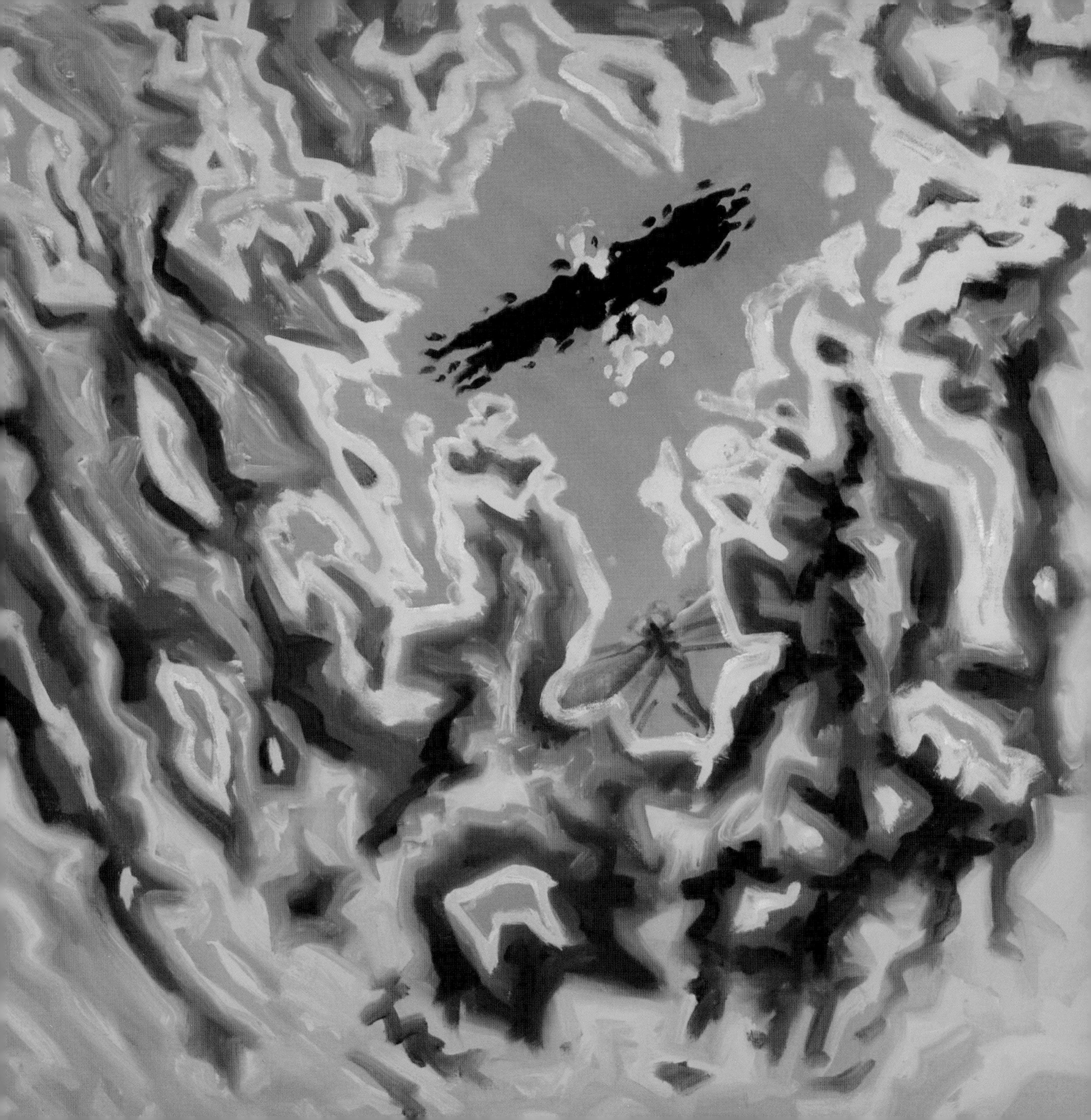

Larry's days were busy feeding Larry Junior, placing the flesh of fish and small animals into Larry Junior's gaping mouth. Soon enough, Larry Junior was large enough to flap his wings tentatively, letting the breeze catch the underside and riffle the wing tips. But, Larry grew apprehensive, because his son was ungainly and gangly. He could only watch helplessly as Larry Junior awkwardly teetered on the edge of the nest, flailed wildly, and then plummeted in a flurry of feathers and twigs and leaves through the branches toward the river.

Bob looked up to see a flash of feathers tumbling end over end into the water. Without thinking, he darted up to the surface and arrived just as Larry Junior hit the water. Bob pushed up hard underneath him, trying to balance the awkward bird on his back as he swam toward the shore. A sodden Larry Junior scrambled onto the shore shaking wildly.

As Larry swooped down to his son, he raised a wing to Bob to thank him. Bob dipped his head slightly and silently swam away.

The leaves in the trees around the broad river were turning a brilliant mosaic of red and orange and yellow, signaling the coming of winter and cool breezes. Bob felt a sense of pride that so many of his little ones had survived to swim away into the river to fend for themselves. But his accomplishment felt bittersweet, because he knew he would never raise a batch of fry again.

Up in the trees, Larry watched his young one fly away. He knew that Larry Junior had survived because of Bob's quick thinking and bravery.

Bob thought of how to avoid his fate, but he knew that any plan he hatched wouldn't satisfy the hunger of the eagle and would result in the death of another fish. He spent his last day visiting his favorite nooks in the river, where the sunlight broke into a thousand pieces and caused the rock gravel to shimmer. He dipped in and out of the currents that carried him like a water ride. He turned over to swim on his back and stared up into the sky instead of down onto the riverbed. At the end of the day, he swam slowly toward the flat rock where Larry had dropped him back into the water.

As Bob swam up to the rock, he saw Larry staring intently into the rippling water. Larry had been sure that Bob would not come.

As Bob's head broke through the surface, he bravely looked directly into Larry's eyes.

Larry cleared his throat, "I can't eat you! I came to thank you for saving Larry Junior. I searched for you before, but I couldn't tell which flash in the river was you." Bob took a deep breath and sighed with relief.

"I've seen you flying above me," Bob admitted. "What freedom you have."

"I never thought of it that way," Larry said. "I always fly alone, so I've never talked to anyone about it."

Bob pondered, "I'm always around other fish, but sometimes I like to swim my own way. Even when I'm around the other fish, I still feel pretty alone."

Larry shuffled his talons around on the rock and prepared to fly off, "Well, I'll just stop by this rock every so often, if you care to stop by too." And he flew away.

For the next few years, through the seasons of cold and wind, and warmth and breezes, Bob and Larry would meet at the rock and chat. They talked about life in the sky and life in the water and why eagles don't fly in flocks or why independent fish were "unusual."

Every so often, there would be a day of such striking beauty that they stared in awe at the stretch of river, trees, and sky around them, tilting their heads in unison as a slight change in breeze or flash of light caused a new twist or sparkle.

Now, Larry often hovered over the flat rock hoping that Bob would poke his head above the ripples for a chat.

Some days, they traveled upriver together, Bob swimming mightily against the strong current upstream, trying to avoid Larry's shadow. Together they would return, Bob successfully darting away from Larry's shadow when he was aided by the current.

After many years, Bob noticed he couldn't dart through the water as fast as he used to, and his fins had become a little ragged. He rarely explored his favorite nooks and crevices anymore, and his marathon swims with Larry grew more difficult. Bob knew that he needed to set his fish affairs in order. He swam some formations with the fingerlings and took some trips with the other fish, enjoying the whoosh of the water and the drafting effect of their synchronized swim.

But, Bob needed to talk to Larry.

“Bob, you’ve lost your sparkle,” said Larry one day as they visited at their rock. Bob sucked deeply into his gills and said ruefully, “My friend, my time here is short. I’m not the feisty young fish I used to be, and I have a favor to ask of you.

“The first time we met, even as scared as I was, it was an amazing feeling soaring through the air. I saw our river, our whole world, as just a small piece of a bigger world all laid out from above,” Bob continued. “And I have dreamed every day of feeling that feeling of flying again.”

Bob ducked under the water quickly to catch a gill-full of breath and to calm himself. As he emerged, he asked, "Larry, will you fly me above the river one more time?"

Larry turned his head away quickly. He didn't want Bob to see his predator eyes get teary. He quickly swung his head back around to nod yes, "I would be happy to fly one more time with you, Bob."

Larry tenderly curled his talons around Bob's belly, forming a sling to hoist Bob into the air. With a mighty whoosh, Larry lifted off and soared into the clouds.

As Bob looked down along the stretch of river, he observed the golds and oranges of turning leaves and felt the breath of the breezes against his scales. He reflected on the beauty of where he had swum and on his friendship with Larry, the only other creature who really understood him.

Larry also was thinking about his friendship with Bob and how his typical flight over the river was special because he could share it with his friend. Larry's heart was full with his appreciation for Bob.

Bob held his breath as best he could, but soon the layer of water embracing his scales had stretched into thin threads and flew off him, leaving him dry.

Bob began to struggle in discomfort, so Larry swooped back down to the river, wistful that their mutual trip was ending.

Larry dipped his white head sadly as he released Bob back into the river. Bob waved a jaunty fin to Larry and dove down into the water.

Then Bob stopped swimming, let the river current buoy him up, cradle him, and carry him away.

And though Larry recounted these events many times over many years, only Larry Junior knew the story wasn't just a fish tale.

The End

The dragonfly is a beautiful insect with two pairs of strong transparent iridescent wings and large multifaceted eyes. Dragonflies live near streams, pools, and rivers and are found on every continent except Antarctica. Dragonflies are predators who eat other harmful insects like mosquitos. Adult dragonflies do not bite or sting humans although young dragonflies may deliver a harmless bite. Some dragonflies may live as long as 7 years.

Karen Schaufeld is the co-founder of All Ages Read Together, a program dedicated to educating children in need with free preschool programs in their communities. Karen has three children and resides in Leesburg, Virginia, with her husband, Fred, and two dogs. *Larry and Bob* is her second book.

Learn more at www.quidnepress.org

Kurt Schwarz is a realist painter specializing in portraiture, still life, and landscape. The exploration of color harmony and spatial concepts are equally important in Schwarz's creations. His skill in capturing the complex nature of his subjects has contributed to his reputation of being one of Loudoun County's finest artists. Kurt's career highlights include six solo exhibitions and publication in fine art magazines, including the international publication, *The American Artist.*

Learn more at www.kurtschwarz.com